LOLO'S SUPERPOWER

BY LESLIE PITT

ILLUSTRATED BY ASHLEY RADES

ISBN 13: 978-1-63489-163-9
Library of Congress Catalog Number: 2018954473
Printed in the United States of America
First Printing: 2018
22 21 20 19 18   5 4 3 2 1

Cover and book design by Mayfly Design

Minneapolis, MN
www.wiseinkpub.com

To order, visit www.itascabooks.com or call 1-800-901-3480.
Reseller discounts available.

Acknowledgments – While there are so many to acknowledge, I humbly thank you all: Amy Cutler Quale, with Wise Ink, for sharpening my vision to broaden this book's message; Linda Williams, for selflessly motivating me; Lisa Cartwright, whose lifelong friendship sparked this book; and Louise Duff, my twin cousin, to whom I first confided the idea of Lolo.

Thank you all so very much.

Dedication – To children who see themselves as themselves and who know no obstacle is too large, this book is dedicated to you.

To Mom, Dad, and Greg, this book is my loving tribute to each of you and to all of you, for giving me my superpower to soar with your endless love and support.

And to all the loving souls who have been part of this incredible journey, this thing I call "life."

I cannot thank you enough.

Lolo was a doll who lived in a toy store. Lolo lived alone on the very bottom shelf while lots and lots of other dolls lived on the other shelves.

Lolo didn't really look like the other dolls. You see, all of the other dolls kind of looked like the children who visited them in the toy store.

There were dolls with long hair, short hair, and no hair at all.

There were dolls of all different shapes and sizes, too.

And then there was Lolo.

First of all, Lolo was blue. Yes, blue—just like the color of the sky, the water, and the globe. But Lolo liked that because none of the other dolls were blue.

Lolo was soft and squishy, just like a big hug. Lolo liked that, too.

Lolo had a left arm and a right arm. And Lolo had a right leg and a left leg. These arms and legs had snaps! They could come on and off whenever Lolo wanted. None of the other dolls could do that.

But what Lolo really loved was being so different than all of the other dolls—
it was a superpower, no less. Lolo loved having a superpower.

Every day, Lolo woke up with a big smile and gave a great, big Lolo smile to all of the children looking for their forever friend.

Lolo imagined what life with a forever friend would be like. They would go on great adventures together. They would visit the ocean and splash in the water. They would ride bikes to places far, far away. And they would build forest castles out of pine cones and tree branches. Best of all, they would always be there for each other, no matter what.

Every day, the other dolls were picked by their forever friends.

But Lolo did not get picked.

Sometimes, Lolo would hear the other dolls say things about Lolo.
They would say,

"Lolo will never get picked!"

"That Lolo doesn't even look like us!"

"Lolo is too blue, and has those silly snaps!"

It made Lolo sad to hear this. But Lolo knew that being different and not looking like any of the other dolls was a superpower. Lolo's forever friend would love Lolo's superpower with all of the blueness and squishiness— and the snaps, too!

One day, Lolo woke up and waited on the bottom shelf with that big Lolo grin. Lolo waited and waited, but no one came to play. The day was almost over when Lolo saw a boy and a girl walk up to the dolls.

"Lucy, are you excited for your birthday party?" the little boy asked.

Lucy looked sad. "I don't really feel like having a birthday this year, Greg."

"But you love your birthday! The candles, the cake, and the party with our whole family and your best friends! What happened?" he asked.

Lucy got sad. "I just don't feel like myself anymore since I got my new leg. I'm different from everybody. "

Greg hugged his sister. "You're still you, Lucy—you have superpowers now! Your new leg is silver and shiny! And the best part is that you can take it off and put it back on, whenever you want. That makes you different from the rest of us! That's YOUR superpower!"

But Lucy still looked sad. That's when Greg saw Lolo smiling up at him and took Lolo off the shelf.

"Lucy, look at this blue doll! Have you ever seen a doll with snaps like these?"

But Lucy was too sad and she started to cry. Greg put Lolo back on the shelf and took Lucy's hand, and they walked away. As they left the toy store, Greg looked back at Lolo.

The next day, Lolo's smile wasn't as big as usual. Lolo had been hoping that Lucy would be a forever friend.

Lolo tried really, really hard to think about all the reasons to be happy. Lolo thought about being squishy and blue and having snaps. But Lolo was too sad and wondered if being *so* different from the other dolls was really such a superpower, after all.

Then, Lolo heard a familiar voice talking to the toy store owner. "Excuse me, sir, I want to get that blue, squishy doll for my sister."

Lolo slowly started to smile.

"Do you mean this one? This is Lolo," said the man as he reached down to the bottom shelf.

"Yes, Lolo is my sister's forever friend. I just know it," said Greg. He gave Lolo a squishy hug.

When they walked away from the shelves, Lolo looked back at the other dolls and knew that being different was the exact reason Lolo was chosen. Lolo smiled.

At home, Greg handed the doll to his sister.
"Happy birthday, Lucy!" he said. "This is Lolo."

"Is this the blue doll from the toy store? The one with the snaps?" she said. Lucy hugged and hugged Lolo's soft, blue squishiness with all her might. "Look, look! Lolo's leg can come off just like my leg can! We both have superpowers because we are different!" said Lucy with a giggle.

That's when Lolo finally knew that Lucy was a forever friend. Lolo also knew that real forever friends choose you because of what makes you different, and being different is a special superpower.

The End

ABOUT THE AUTHOR

Leslie Pitt has been called a "globe-trotting humanitarian," but she started out as a little girl who dreamed of making the world a better place. She is educated in law, nursing, global health, and human rights. After a twenty-five-year career in healthcare, Leslie shifted paths to pursue her passion to help children with differing abilities by starting the global nonprofit organization Project Lolo.

When Leslie was six, she lost her left leg above the knee—she knows what it is like to be a child longing to be seen for who she really is, beyond her differing physical abilities. She wrote *Lolo's Superpower* to help children embrace differing abilities that make them unique.

Leslie lives near Lake of the Isles in Minneapolis, Minnesota, close to her family. She shares her space with two well-loved cats, Aksel and Oskar.

ABOUT THE ILLUSTRATOR

Ashley Rades is an illustrator living and working in Minnesota. She has lived in Minnesota nearly all of her life and takes time to enjoy all that the state has to offer. She is a true Minnesotan at heart and spends a lot of time outdoors. Camping, canoeing, or hiking with friends and family are some of her favorite pastimes.

Ashley is driven by her desire to tell stories and sees illustration as a powerful way to tackle big ideas. She was inspired as a child by children's books such as *The Giving Tree* and *Good Dog, Carl*. Ever since, her art has grown from sketches in the margins of her schoolwork to a professional career. She feels that there are a lot of important stories out there to be told and hopes that through her work a few of them can come to life.

ABOUT PROJECT LOLO

Project Lolo is a global nonprofit organization that believes all children should have equal standing in life, regardless of differing abilities. Its mission is to embrace the steadfast empowerment of all children, and to provide access to orthopedic care and orthopedic devices such as prostheses or wheelchairs to help them live limitlessly. To learn more, please visit **www.ProjectLolo.org**.